Play-a-Sound™

The Scary Monster House

Illustrations by Michael Carroll

Publications International, Ltd.

This is the house
where Frank lives.

This is the owl
who hoots in the night,

In the tree by the house
where Frank lives.

This is the window
    that glows green light,

And shines on the owl
    who hoots in the night,

In the tree by the house
    where Frank lives.

This is the mummy
whose rags are a sight,

And get caught in the door
when it bangs shut tight,

Next to the window
that glows green light,

And shines on the owl
who hoots in the night,

In the tree by the house
where Frank lives.

This is the black cat
   who yowls with delight,

At the mummy whose rags
   are a dreadful sight,

When they get caught
   in the door shut tight,

Next to the window
   that glows green light,

And shines on the owl
   who hoots in the night,

In the tree by the house
   where Frank lives.

This is the wolf man who
jumps and takes flight,

When he hears the cat
who yowls with delight,

At the mummy whose rags
are a dreadful sight,

When they get caught
in the door shut tight,

Next to the window
that glows green light,

And shines on the owl
who hoots in the night,

In the tree by the house
where Frank lives.

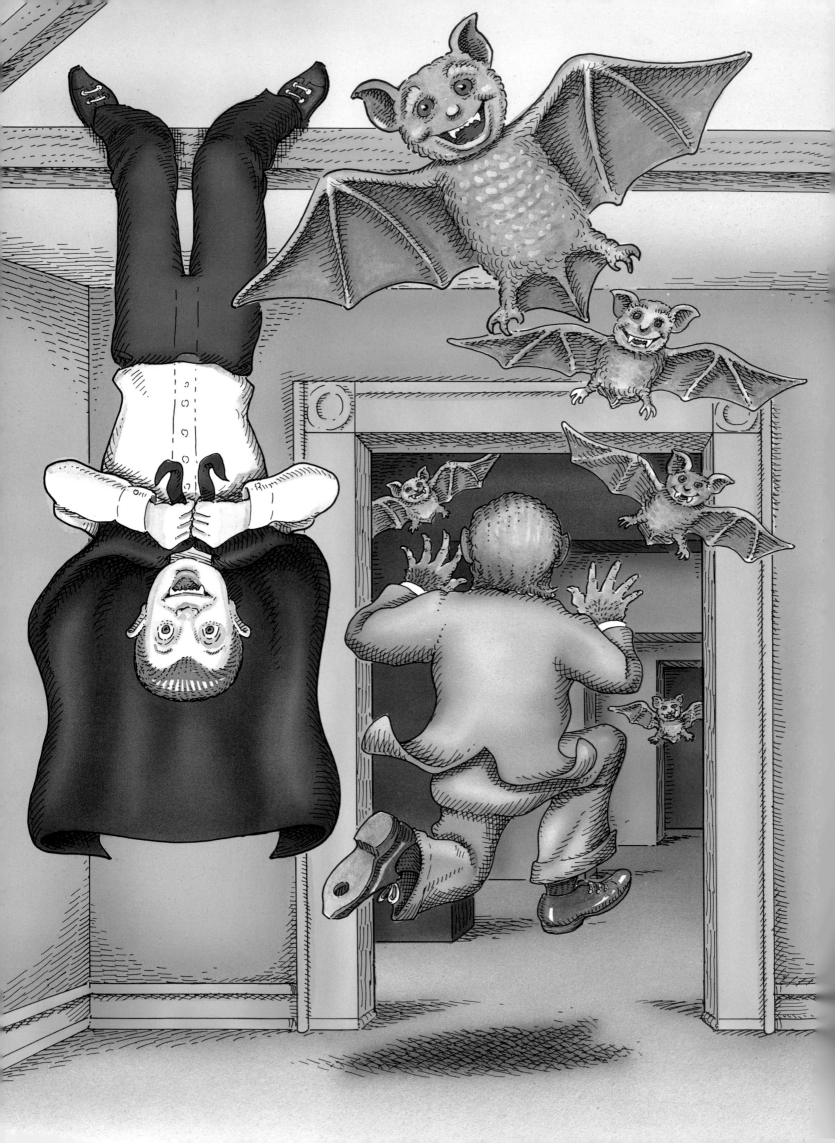

These squeaky bats
  are hanging on tight,

Over the wolf man
  as he takes flight,

When he hears the cat
  who yowls with delight,

At the mummy whose rags
  are a dreadful sight,

When they get caught
  in the door shut tight,

Next to the window
  that glows green light,

And shines on the owl
  who hoots in the night,

In the tree by the house
  where Frank lives.

These banging shutters
will give you a fright,

And wake up the bats
who hang on tight,

Over the wolf man
as he takes flight,

When he hears the cat
who yowls with delight,

At the mummy whose rags
are a dreadful sight,

When they get caught
in the door shut tight,

Next to the window
that glows green light,

And shines on the owl
who hoots in the night,

In the tree by the house
where Frank lives.

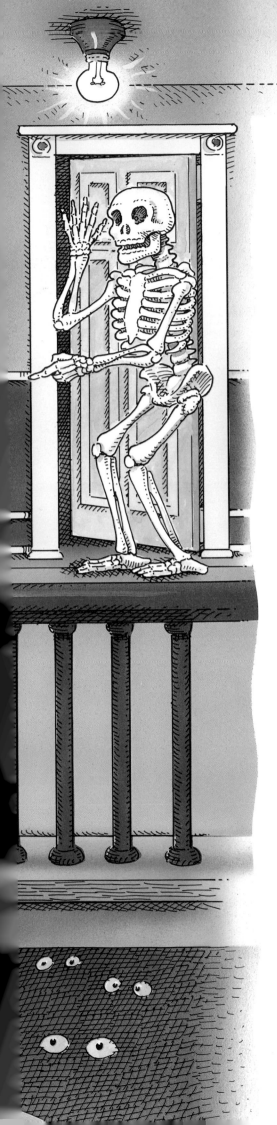

Go down the hall—
    make a left, then a right.

What is there? Who can say?
    Will it growl? Will it bite?

Run past the shutters
    that give you a fright,

And wake up the bats
    who hang on tight,

Over the wolf man
    as he takes flight,

When he hears the cat
    who yowls with delight,

At the mummy whose rags
    are a dreadful sight,

When they get caught
    in the door shut tight,

Next to the window
    that glows green light,

And shines on the owl
    who hoots in the night,

In the tree by the house
    where Frank lives.

Suddenly, there is a very strange sight.
It's Frank on his way to fly his new kite.
He asks, "Like to come?"
I say, "Yes, I might!"
And out we go, into the dark night,
Ready to fly Frank's outrageous new kite.